Carter

Contents

Introduction

This series of short stories was bourne out of love for the Author's spouse. Their long standing relationship holds no secrets and opens the door to true intimacy.

Intimate

/ˈɪntɪmət/

adjective

1. closely acquainted; familiar.

"intimate friends"

2. private and personal.

"intimate details of his sexual encounters"

Hypnosis

"I'll try my best not to fall asleep." she whispered as she swung her weary legs onto the bed.

"Just lay there and relax, it's my turn to do the work and I've had a bit of an idea. Put that blindfold on".

Anne rolled her eyes but gave a wry smile, she knew that Stan would always take care of her needs Even after all this time their sex life was probably more colourful than most peoples and they had manged to keep their kinky secrets just between them.

"This evening", Stan whispered gruffly, "You will listen to my voice and my voice only. You will not move, but you will not be bound. Do you understand?"

"Yes Sir!" Anne responded softly, under her breath as she would with their normal activities.

"There is no 'Sir' here, I am your guide, just listen.

The room was dark, but the familiar feel of the soft mattress and duvet below her was comforting. It wasn't often that she would lay naked, unclothed for any period of time, so this felt a little strange even in their most intimate times. Stan placed a hand either side of her head, being careful not to trap her long brown hair underneath his hands and leaned in to her. He kissed her deeply enough to ignite the fire that had been burning in his groin all day.

"I Love you" he told her, before standing and manoeuvring to his side of the bed. She felt his weight bear down on the other side of the bed, and only by the small candle he had lit earlier, he gazed over naked body with pure admiration. He thought to himself *She is incredible!*

"Shall we begin?"

"OK". She sighs with anticipation. Internally she thinks to herself

What on earth is he doing? Does he think he's some sort of hypnotist? It's very cold in here, my nipples are a bit sore. Oh, I must remember to put the laundry in the dryer before I settle for the night. Oh, He's talking...

"Ok listen to my voice". It's calm and deep without a real bass to it but familiar to her.

"Hear my calmness and focus on your breathing. I want you to concentrate on each breath, feeling it draw into you, notice how it feels cool in your nose and at the back of your throat and the swell of your lungs as you inhale deeply to your diaphragm, and the warmth as you exhale through your mouth, feeling it on your lips. I want you to breath in to my count. 1-2-3-4-5-6-7. And exhale to my count 1-2-3-4-5-6-7-8-9-10. Empty your lungs on each breath. Feel it and concentrate on it."

She stifles a laugh as he begins to count, but tags along for the ride anyway. Her breathing slows to his count, and she settles into her guided instruction.

"Concentrate only on your breathing"

He can see the silhouette of her naked body against the candle light. Her large breasts, fallen to her sides slightly as she rests, rising and falling gently to his timings. He runs his eyes down her stomach and can see her pubic hair protruding slightly. It's been week or two since she made him get the trimmers out. She loves to be trimmed and tidy down there, it's an intimate act that has a practical use too!

After a few minutes of concentrated breathing, Stan speaks slightly louder now, and with a more confident tone.

"I'm going to count to ten. When I reach 3, I want you to make sure you are comfortable with your legs slightly parted and hands by your side, motionless. And when I get to ten you are going to imagine opening your eyes and laying in a pitch-black room".

She continues to breath

IN 1-2-3

"ONE"

4-5-6

"TWO"

7 – Out 1-2-3

"THREE" Anne slightly parts her legs as instructed and places her hands by her sides.

4-5-6

"FOUR" Stan can see the dark line of her pussy through the hair in the candlelight

7-8-9

"FOUR"

10-IN-1-2

"FIVE, SIX, SEVEN" Anne stops counting her breaths, and feels apprehension for the first time in a long time

What if this isn't what I think it is?" she monologues

"EIGHT, NINE, TEN"

In her mind's eye she visualises as instructed, being in a pitch-black room laying as she is now. Stan goes on.

"You are in a dark room, laid on a bed, Naked. To your right is a solitary candle, casting dim light onto a brick wall. The room is cool but comfortable. It feels like a cave, and distantly you can hear drips into invisible puddles." Anne visualises as best she can, and feels a little frightened. She never really liked the dark much, but then she's never told Stan that so how would he know?

"You can feel a light yet warm breeze across your body, it stiffens your nipples as it touches them".

He blows gently onto her nipples, and she's unsure on whether its real or in her head, but they react never the less.

"Amidst the silence, you hear the loud bolt of a door opening somewhere in the direction of your head end, and it closes." Stan slams the bedroom door startling Anne; She jumps in place.

"You hear footsteps walk slowly along the floor, proper shoes clicking along in slow cadence, click click, click."

Oh shit, I'm in! She thinks to herself as she realises, she unwittingly become a victim of her own imagination. She can literally hear a man's shoe walking towards her, yet she knows she lying on her bed at home.

"The footsteps stop by your head. If you could look up, you'd see a dark shadowed figure standing over you" Stan continues.

"He places his hands on your shoulders, they're warm yet soft" Anne imagines the stranger's hands on her naked body.

"He surveys you, and he touches you at the point where his gaze falls upon you". Gently, Stan runs a finger over her body. Tracing a line from her lips, tenderly down her neck to her right nipple. Then across to her left, down her stomach to her hairy mound. He stops just before the crease of her quim begins. She shudders with goosebumps.

Her mind is telling her that this stranger is tall, with a brimmed hat and one of those plague doctor type masks with a beak. No-one put this in her head, so where's it coming from?

This is too real she internalises.

"You realise that you are tied to the bed, your hands, legs and arms are fixed in place." Anne imagines trying to move, but her body is still she can't move, yet no-one has physically restrained her

"The stranger touches your pussy; he asks you a question and expects an answer... IS IT WET?"

"Yes" Anne replies sheepishly. The breathing deeply has made her throat dry. She is imagining a strong hand between her legs; she can feel the warmth of it, yet nothing at all, and suddenly she realises that her pussy is actually wet.

“The Stranger waves with a motion of his hand, and another set of footsteps appear, this time it sounds like heels”.

Anne imagines a slender woman walking towards them in a pant suit, powerfully dressed yet feminine in every way. Dark haired again.

“The heels stop by your head again and you feel an instant light touch on both of your nipples”

Stan is now touching her nipples as he speaks. A delicate middle finger on each and Anne gasps for breath; unsure of what are real sensations and what are fantasy.

“The woman continues to manipulate your nipples it is relentless” Stan has given himself permission to play with her tits as always. He is somewhat obsessed with them, even to the point where a few of his close friends have seen pictures of them, unbeknownst to Anne.

“The stranger is at your waist. You feel him start to stroke your pubic hair with his fingers, while your nipples are still being caressed.” Anne takes a deep breath as she imagines this masked stranger stroking her.

“He admires you, and with his stray hand, begins to touch you elsewhere. Your legs, stomach hips etc.” Anne can already feel the imaginary touch. Imagination is never something she’s had a problem with.

“He instructs the woman now to step away and unties only your hands. He places them onto your tits and tells you “KEEP THEM STIMULATED UNTIL I TELL YOU OTHERWISE””. Anne places her own hands onto her breasts as if being placed by an invisible force. *This is Weird* she thinks as her fingers tenderly touch her breast as only, she can do; almost against her own will.

“The stranger cups your pussy with his hand, you feel his warmth cover it once again, but this time he runs his finger along your wetness from bottom to top and he starts to use your own lubrication to stimulate your clit. It starts to pulse and you feel your lips relax as if yearning to be filled."

Oh god I can feel someone touching my clit! Anne has a mini panic because she knows there is no one else there. Her pussy starts to pulse with the imaginary circling of her little bean. All the while her own fingers dance seductively over her own curvy bosom, seemingly guided by ghostly hands.

"The stranger enjoys you; he enjoys seeing your naked form before him, he wants you. His finger digresses south and starts to hover and stroke your hairy entrance with his middle two fingers."

Anne writhes on the bed now, anxious flicking her own nipples, imagining the top hatted stranger with his hand between her legs, touching her as she loves to be touched by her husband, and yet, by no one.

"With his free hand the stranger unties your legs, you're free to move, but he tells you to "STAY WHERE YOU ARE"".

Anne's legs suddenly come to life as if a weight has been taken off of them, she parts them more, exposing her very wet and glistening snatch in the candle light. Stan can see just how wet he is as he moved to look at her from the foot end. He's hard himself now.

"He places his hand firmly over your twat and looks you in the eye. As he does, he plunges his two middle fingers deep inside of you, his hot palm presses firmly on your clit, and with a hooked finger motion, he starts to move his hand up and down and in and out! He gets faster and faster".

Oh god, I can't take it much more"

Annes body is writhing as she is still working her own nips as instructed, her legs are spreadeagled as she imagines the stranger fingering her, and she starts to feel the pressure build up inside her.

Knowing his wife, Stan interjects.

"The stranger instructs you firmly "DO NOT ORGASM". But his fingers remain relentless"

Stan can see his wife's cunt pulsing; he knows she's ready.

"The stranger says to you "WHEN I TOUCH YOUR CLIT, YOU MAY ORGASM".

Stan stands and silently steps toward the bed, Anne still squirming delightfully. He leans forwards and stealthily with his first finger hovering over her clitoris, He watches her closely. The moment approaches and he can see the physical tension in her body. She trembles continuously and lightly he touches her button. He was not expecting the result!

As soon as his finger brushed her tender and swollen clit, she screamed! Her back arched, and her legs slammed shut. She shook for about 30 secs violently, as if seizing, and Stam seriously considered calling an ambulance! After the seizing, all her muscles relax and her bladder can no longer hold. She involuntarily soaks their bed in warm piss. Stan realised she was still in a state of hypnosis.

"Listen to my voice!" I will count back from ten and when I get to zero, you'll awake in our bed!

TEN, NINE, EIGHT, SEVEN, SIX, FIVE, FOUR, THREE, TWO, ONE, ZERO.

Silence, save for heavy breathing.

Stan removed Annes blindfold. He looked he in the eye and she looked at him back!

"Where, In the holy fuck, did you learn to do that?? I feel like I've done ten rounds with Mike Tyson!" she laughed and cried at the same time, like a marathon runner completing an endurance race,

"Erm, I just read I bit of an article on the power of meditation and thought I'd see if it worked! I wanted to you be relaxed, not explode!" Stan chuckled. Anne Looked at him, tears running down her face.

"So, what was you?"

"What?"

"I couldn't tell who if anyone was touching me, I mean you obviously did the fingering".

"Actually, I didn't, I only traced my finger down you and played with your tits a bit, all the rest was in your head"

"So, you got nothing?"

"Not yet!"

"Give me a minute". Anne struggled off the bed towards the bathroom. Stan checked her ass out as always. He called through

"I'll be surprised if you've got any pee left, did you not see the bed?" he laughed!

"I haven't" she called back.

She staggered back through using the wall for support. Stan laid on the bed, naked, with his fairly impressive hard on still raging. Anne always thought she was lucky he was so well endowed! She knew her friend Diane's husband wasn't so big, as they'd secretly shared some conversation and showed each other pictures in the past. *Poor Woman* she used to think.

She crawled slowly onto the wet bed, and laid back in the mess. Something they always did before the post sex scoop and clean up. She put her head on his nearly middle-aged spreading stomach.

"I love you, but I think you may have decommissioned me for a few days"

"Is that so? We shall see!"

With that, she grasped his impressive shaft by the base, her hand span was just under half the length of his penis, and he was circumcised, so his head always appeared bigger than most anyway. She looked at it for a moment and considered Diane's husband again *Imagine only having that for the rest of your life* she mused as she started to run her tongue around his head of his large cock.

He sighed and placed his hands behind his head like he always does when she sucks him. She started expertly with her tongue, licking lightly and gently, tickling his eye with the tip of her tongue before taking the shaft of his dick and kissing along its length. She enjoyed this part the most, but secretly it reminded her of a cartoon dog with a bone. Sometimes shed even bite it, Stan was akin to a bit of pain. She caressed his swollen balls with her right hand, as she then took his whole length in her mouth. She'd been practicing deep throating for over a year now, at Stans request and finally mastered it. Slowly she coaxed him along, taking her time, speeding up, slowing down and all the while looking him in the eye. She wanted to return tonight's favour, so he wasn't cumming just yet!

She stopped and instructed him to lie on his back, he complied. She stood over him and he could see her sleek yet hairy womanhood. He didn't mind the hair at all, in fact sometime preferred it. He had always admired that even though they had three beautiful children together, her pussy never looked worn out or over stretched, even with the cut & forceps from number 3.

She stroked herself as she stood atop him, and now a few minutes has passed, she let her bladder go under control this time, covering him as he so loved. She than squatted over his face, her curvy figure showing of all the more to him, and spoke

"Clean it up for me". She cupped the side of his head lovingly and put her full weight onto his face smothering him with her juices and her piss. His hard on was ready to burst now. All this in one night? He couldn't believe his luck. She released him for air,

"Let me fuck you!" he gasped, holding her ass from underneath, still wanting every last taste of her. She stood up and turned around, then fell to her knees facing away from him. Bent over like that, her cunt, and arse were on full display, he loved to see the little skin tag she had on her perineum.

And she lowered her womanly form onto his large, hard cock. He felt every inch of it sliding slowly into her, almost enough to blow his load there and then. She began to work her wet pussy on him, bouncing expertly like a pole dancing porn star. Twerking on it, sliding on it and adjust the pace to keep him clueless. She was most definitely in control now.

As she fucked him, she grunted,

"Maybe.......You should.....go..........and......do..a......hypnosis....course.......so .....you....can.........make...me...........cum.....OH GOD!............ALL THE...... FUUUUCK!!!!..........TIIIMMEE!" Another mind-blowing orgasm for Anne has got to be a record for this year at least. She slowed down and slumped, him still inside her.

"I don't know if I can go any more my love" she whimpered, feeling completely spent.

"Lay back and think of England then!"

"Okay". She giggled as she rolled over, and he knelt his considerable hulk over her, his hard cock still raging for his wife. He bent forward and as he entered her, spreading her open, and kissed her deeply. Her clitoris incredibly sensitive now, rubbing against his pubis, she continued to shudder and writhe as he starts to pound her. Lifting her legs up and holding them apart by the ankles while he took his wife hard, fast and deep. The headboard banging now against the wall.

"Shhh!" She whispered,

"Come on, fill me up!" His back arched and his grip on her ankles tightened. His balls squeezed and he exploded his seed into her as he'd done so many times before. He collapsed on top of her, his big shoulders covering her whole body.

He pulled his still hard cock from her, very satisfied hole and his load followed it back out, down her slit onto the bed. She laid looking up at the ceiling, as he rolled over next to her.

"I love you" he told her,

"I love you too! Shower?"

Resignation

"I CAN'T DO THIS; CAN'T DO THIS ANYMORE. FUCK YOU AND FUCK YOUR JOB!!" she shouted through into the Merc's Bluetooth system. Fighting a full-blown melt down, she pulled in to a lay-by through blurred, teary eyes. Pulling up the parking brake button, the little (P) told her she was safe, she put the car into PARK and begun to cry into her hands. 5 years she put into that firm, and never took time off. She could probably be a partner in another year or so, if she hadn't just told them what she did! The phone rang through the sound system again and flashed on the dashboard.

STAN.

"I got your text, what's going on?" He sounded worried, yet calm and reassuring.

"I've walked out! I can't work for that disgusting old perv anymore! I'm so sorry, I know it's going to affect us all!"

"Babe, what happened?"

"He told me that I "should have won the Marriott case, and that maybe my fat arse would be better served dancing on a pole, rather than pretending to be a solicitor!"

"What the fuck?! I'll rip his fucking head off! Where are you anyway, I'm nearly home?"

"I just pulled over, I'm still half hour away." She was breathing shallowly, still fighting her emotion.

"Right, well, just take a minute and drive home safely. I'll see you there."

Anne's journey home was a little better after the phone call from her husband. Nothing has changed, but he always had a calming tone in his voice. She had never known him to panic in 15 years. He has soothed her for now and she know she will be able to sound things out with him. For now, at least she's calm. She pulls onto the gravel in front of their home, and parked next to Stan's 5 series giving herself enough space to step out of her little two-seater.

She pushes the handle for the front door down and the old oak swings away from her into the hall way. The warmth hits her quickly. *Jesus! It's hot in here*. She kicks her sensible shoes somewhere near the shoe rack and they fall with a soft thud.

"Helloooo?!" She calls out

"Hey! I'm upstairs!" Stan down calls down to her. Dumping her bag on the wooden unit, she heads up the stairs slowly.

"It's very quiet, where are the kids?"

"We'll, as it happens, Mum called at lunch time and asked if they could stay at theirs. I think her and dad want to take them for dinner and cinema, she said we can join them for breakfast with them in the morning about 9.30."

"Oh, right. I thought we were going to do that with them this evening."

"Yeah, do you feel like going out for dinner with kids arguing, and going to watch a kids film?" She smiled and admitted,

"Not really. So, what are we doing instead then?"

The day had darkened already, and the cloudy sky was virtually black outside. Stan flicked the bedroom light on.

"Come and see!" She rolled her eyes at him and reluctantly followed. He led her through the bedroom into their en-suite bathroom. It was lit by candle light, and the bath was full, brimming with bubbles. The scent of Radox filled the room.

"For you. Relax, soak, chill!" I'll be back in a moment.

She lets out a sigh and looks at her self through the light condensation on the mirror noticing her mascara has smudged a little. *I hope Stan didn't see that!* She began to slowly unbutton her pink silk blouse. Stan love this one as it made her tits stand out a little more than usual. She allowed the open front to fall away from her, revealing the white laced bra underneath and slipped it off her shoulders allowing it to fall to the floor. She moved to the black pencil skirt, she liked the way it framed her hips and butt. Sliding the zip down at the back it also fell to meet the blouse. The white lace thong matched the bra. The back of it arching over each of her round pert cheeks, meeting together in the middle creating a point that traced down her crack. She reached behind herself and expertly u clipped the clasp on the back of her bra and peeled it away from her body. It was relief! She cupped her breasts and rubbed them firmly, as she did every time she took a bra off. *Ahh that end of the day feeling.* Finally, she bent forwards as she removed her panties and was stood naked, illuminated only by candle light in the warm, black marble bathroom. She looked around momentarily at the beauty of it. *We've done alright for ourselves!*

She dipped her toe carefully into the bath. Knowing her husband well, he had a tendency to run it hot enough to scald your average person. He hadn't, it was hot, but not uncomfortable. Anne always enjoyed getting into a bath and always tried to savour it by doing it slowly. Especially when she's alone. She placed her left foot in, followed by her right. Feeling the hot water around her feet she prepared for her favourite bit, feeling the hot water level cover her slowly. She knelt forward, slowly sinking her lower legs below the surface placing her knees on the bottom beneath the bubbles. They tickled the backs of her legs and she slowly sat back onto her heels she savoured the water level rising slowly over her smooth legs, and gently, lightly it kissed her pussy. It felt hot as it swelled over her modesty, covering her behind to her lower back. She was almost in. She brought her legs out from under her, taking hold of the chrome handles each side and lowered slowly back to lay in the hot water. She watched as her tits begun to float in the deep bath, and gasped as her nipples finally disappeared below the water line. She closed her eyes and tried to relax.

After what felt like an eternity, Anne was startled by a clink of glass next to her ear. She opened her eyes to see Stan sat on the edge of the bath having placed a glass of red wine next to her. He was holding one himself, and took a sip.

"You're very beautiful, you know" it made her blush a touch.

"Thank you." She smiled back to him.

"I thought you might like to relax"

"It's very welcome! Thank you." He leaned forward to kiss her.

"I love you" he told her as their lips separated once again. He stood up and left her to it, leaving the door to their bedroom slightly ajar. Anne took a glug of her wine; half a glass in fact and laid her head back to enjoy the heat of the bath. Her mind started to wander.

Her mind's eye saw her desk in the office. Still covered in paperwork. She saw her scum bag, pervert boss standing in her doorway, letching over her. Her cleavage was showing an inch too much. She imagined squeezing her ample breasts together and telling him he could have them if he begged her! Her imagination flashed forward and he was on his knees begging her to see them, her outfit was now a black lace bodice with a tiny g-string and high boots. Her tits bulging from the top.

She kicked him over onto his back and crushed his tiny dick into his body with her boot. Her mind flashed again. This time it was her on her knees in the same sexy outfit, but a collar and lead lead-ing up to a familiar strong hand. One with the thick gold band she had given him when they were much younger.

Her mind told her that she craved to be used by her husband. Her mind saw him lift her by the throat and pin her to the wall. He kissed her deeply and immediately put three fingers into her.

Her body reacted slowly to her daydream, and her left hand drifted slowly to her nipple, her right hand stroked her pubes tenderly under the comfort of the bubbles. She saw his fingers entering her as if she was watching herself in a porn movie, and with that imagined her left leg suspended by rope level with her shoulder. Suddenly the younger version of Stan not only had three fingers in her

But was forcing an imaginary vibrator onto her little clit. In the real world, she parted her legs and reached down to soothe her deep ache.

She never intended to masturbate, but she couldn't get the image of her husband taking control of her in such a brutal manner out of her head. She laid her head back further, and inserted two fingers into her submerged pussy. She noticed the difference between the hot water and slippery warmth of her insides. She built the tension up quickly, God knows she needed it, they hadn't fucked for nearly a week! And as she felt the pulse in her clit get stronger and the muscles start to clench her fingers, she withdrew. *God, I need some dick.* Resisting the urge to continue, she settles back into the bath, so only her face was exposed to wash her hair.

Out in the bedroom, Stan had brought the wine bottle up with him. A cheap but tasty Merlot from Chile, and placed it on her bedside table. He pulled his Vans T-shirt over his broad shoulders, revealing the old dragon tattoo on his left shoulder blade, folded it in half and draped it over the stool. He dropped his jeans without ceremony, and they hit the cream carpet with a clunk.

"Shit!" *My phone.* He fished it from his jeans, threw it onto the bed, picked folded them once at the waist and sling them over his t-shirt. He stayed wearing his white CK boxers. They were fitted, and slightly see through. His impressive dick resting still soft off to the left and his balls hanging subtly beneath. He clambered onto the bed, flipped himself onto his back, crossed his ankles and put his hands behind his head. Laying on the bed, he listened to the occasional flutter in the water of her moving around in the bath against the silence of their house. He closed his eyes, relaxed and waited.

Anne silently opened their bathroom door by pulling it towards her. Wrapped in a large fluffy blue bath towel, and saw Stan laying in the bed in his underwear. She stood there few a minute silently admiring him. He didn't move save for the steady motion of his chest moving up and down as he dozed. Using a matching towel, she dried her hair off as best she could, and took her time in drying herself off. She always hated being damp after bathing and showering. She stepped in front of her mirror naked, and applied her roll-on deodorant. She went to take a nightie out of her drawer and stopped herself. Looking over at Stan on the bed, she walked over to him in all her glory.

Crawling slowly onto the bed, he rocked slightly as she got closer to him, and she laid her head on his barrel chest. She held her warm skin against his cool body, and wrapped her right leg over his, snuggling into him. Placing a hand on his chest she began to tickle him gently with her finger nails. Goosebumps appeared as he lay sleeping; Stan let out a quiet, satisfied groan.

She turned her attention to his nipples and started to circle them with her finger. She knew he'd always liked have them played with, and today watch no exception. She licked her finger and transferred the moisture to them, blowing making them cold and erect.

Looking down his body as she stimulated his nips, she could she the monster in his white pants start to waken. She could physically see his pulse as his dick grew larger with every beat; moving from his resting place, hanging slightly to the left, to his battle station, stood to attention, front and centre. She loved to watch him grow, and as always fleetingly remembered that not all woman gets to marry such a beast. It struggles against his waist band and gently, so as not to disturb him too much, she lifted it, allowing his large helmet to escape it shackles. She wriggles down and places her head on his stomach. So, her ear is over his navel.

His big friendly giant is almost touching her nose. She stares at it for a few seconds, knowing that she needs it inside her in the not-too-distant future. She feels an ache for him deep in her groin, and notices herself dampen as she moves her legs slightly. She kisses the eye of the beast. It twitches slightly, and she continues to give it slow, tender kisses all over. Anne's kissing speeds up, as she adjusts her position up to her knees and stretches his CK's down under his ball sack, freeing his large scrotum.

She grasps the boys lightly in her right hand and his thick shaft in her left. As she wraps her lips around his purple head, she squeezes with the right and twists slightly with the left. An expert in her craft; she starts slow and deep. The deep throat training they tried had worked and she could take his whole length into her throat. He roused with a gentle breath and he placed his hand on his wife's shoulder to let her know he was both awake and appreciative.

Without extracting his cock from her mouth, she moved and knelt between his legs looking him in the eyes as she skilfully swallowed his length repeatedly.

"That's amazing!" He whispered to his wife. She gave a muffled laugh which tickled his cock a little.

"Did you have a nice bath my love?" He asked her. She came up for air.

"Yes, I was just thanking you for running it for me, because I got a little horny while I was in it!"

She continued to run her hand up and down his shaft as they spoke.

"And what did you think about?"

"Well, I thought about stamping on my bosses' balls first, dressed all slutty but he couldn't have me, then I imagined you had tied me up and were using me roughly."

"That's pretty hot! Come here!" She crawled up him, her smaller frame kneeling over him until she was face to face with him. He enjoyed feeling her large warm breasts hanging and doming to rest on his chest, and he could feel her wetness on his belly as she straddled him. He brought his hands to her face and kissed her deeply.

Her clit came to life as his lips touched hers. It drives her wild when he holds her face and kisses her that way, and she knew what he was doing. He could taste himself in her mouth, and she knew he like to kiss after she'd sucked him. She sometimes enjoyed the same after he'd been down on her.

His hands moved slowly down the soft skin of her back, firmly to start with, and on the return upwards, he tickled her so gently that she shuddered. He felt her nipple harden against him.

His considerable penis was hard and ready, having already been taken care of somewhat, and was resting on Anne's perineum. He could feel her little skin tag just tickle the end of his cock. He could feel her wetness start to drip onto him. She hadn't dripped with excitement for a long time. Her juices felt cold against him. He continued to kiss her as his hands fell on her heart shaped bum.

He pulled her apart gently, and she felt cool air surrounding her usually tucked away inner lips and her tight little asshole. He pulled a bit too hard and her star felt a bit of a sting. She sucked air in through her teeth, but Stan carried on. He lifted her up by her arse and manoeuvred her so that his tip was touching the entrance to her wet quim; she attempted to sit back into it and her rolled his hips into the mattress, denying her. It made her wilder.

"Fuck me!" She commanded.

"When I'm ready!" He grinned as he grabbed her by the hair forcing her to kiss him again, his dick still hovering over her wet hole.

"Argh" she grunted at him and bit his bottom lip as she grew more frustrated.

Stan gathered her damp hair in his hand and began to twist it into a rudimentary pony tail, wrapping it around his strong right hand, pulling it tight. It felt delightfully painful as it tugged from her scalp. He pulled her to his right and off of him, she let out a short-shocked whimper and she hit the mattress on her back. Her Legs were splayed clumsily and her large tits wobbled as her extremely wet slit was displayed to her husband. He continued to pull her hair and forced her to kiss him again as he rolled on top of her. He released and she gasped, only more impassioned. He relaxed her hair and stroked her soft cheek with his hand. His thumb almost doing its own mini stroke on her cheek on. Gazing into her bright blue eyes, he held her attention. She felt, small and vulnerable underneath his large frame, but her groin was commanding her emotions; sexy and wild, her insides ached to receive her husband.

"I love you" he whispered to her as she felt herself clench down there.

Stan knew exactly how to turn his wife on. He had made a quick plan in his head already, and was sticking to it.

"Stop moving!" He told her. And she followed his command immediately. Her arms flopped into a crucifix on the bed but her legs remained bent so her feet were on the duvet with her pussy on full view for him. Her breasts come to rest and fell slightly to the sides of her chest nipples contracted, pointing at the ceiling. Using his left hand, he pushed her chin up forcing her head back exposing her neck and begun to kiss her gently, alternating sides. She felt a drop of her Essence drip from the delicate skin of her womanhood and tickle her cheek as it ran across her skin onto the green tartan duvet. She was over-ready, but Stan wasn't even close.

Kissing her neck, he ran his fingertips across her curves, from her clavicle to her waist, carefully avoiding her nipples. He knew exactly what he was doing, and her tension kept building. His fingers circled back and completed the loop then went again all with his hardness touching her entrance still. This time with two fingers, then three, four and finally his whole hand. It was excruciatingly delicate and Anne was now breathing heavy, moaning and gasping. She snapped at her husband.

"Will you please just fuck me?!"

"I will fuck your when I'm ready, now lie still!" *Oh, fuck he's hot!* She thought to herself.

His cock pulled away from her wet pussy as he started to kiss down onto her chest. Her body was starting to writhe with every slight touch. Her skin felt electrified and she focussed on every little kiss of his lips. He moved his head over to her right breast and kissed all around it; Again, avoid her nipple. He repeated himself on the opposite side, following the round curve of her body with his face close to her. He deliberately caught her nipple with his nose as he returned to centre and her body twitched and she inhaled sharply. *She's nearly ready*, he mused.

Continuing his campaign of kisses, he moved further south. And reached her trimmed mound. He could see the wetness that she had produced for him, and a damp patch was forming under her. He hadn't seen her physically leak with excitement for a long time. Avoiding his wife's neat folds, he kissed her out lips. She thrusted her hips subtly, showing him that she craved to be entered. He kissed his way slowly up her body again, ending as their mouths met once again. She couldn't help herself, and grabbed his head pulling him into her face a kissed him deeply. She felt for his end with her crotch but he wasn't close enough to force him into her. He knew exactly where his dick was pointing and he prepared himself for her to react.

Looking at her lovingly, he ran one single finger down the line of her nose, across her pink lips and down to her neck. She was looking back at him and had relaxed into him touching her seductively. His face changed, became somehow sterner and a flash seemed to cross his eyes it startled her a little. He opened his large, strong hand and clasped her throat gently at first. She bit her bottom lip, she knew what to expect and tipped her head back to expose her whole throat to him.

As he squeezed it, hard, she felt her windpipe close, and started to make short sharp noises from her throat. As her throat closed, she felt her pussy open. His large, hard length was forcing its way into her. It hit her cervix and pushed it inside. She opened her legs as wide as she could to receive as much of him as possible. His heavy balls came to rest on her arse crack.

He didn't move, staying perfectly still inside her, enjoying the warm moistness and watching her face. Still unable to breath, her eyes rolled back into her half and he could see only white. They'd done this a thousand times before and Stan knew exactly what he was waiting for. Then it happened. Just as she was about to lose consciousness her vision started to blacken around the periphery, Stan felt her inner muscles tighten involuntarily around his perfectly still shaft and knew what to do. He released her throat and her vision cleared almost immediately as he withdrew from her about half way, and started to pound his weight into her delicate yet soaking quim. Her spasming cunt gripped him firmly as he slid in and out of her and as she coughed, regaining control of her breathing, she started to feel the pressure build deep within her.

He could see her getting close. Quickly he placed his large hand back onto her throat as he continued fucking her deep and hard, his shaft disappearing rapidly each time deep into her with each thrust.

He squeezed again, while reaching between her legs and rubbing her sensitive pink clit; this time with less tenderness, she made a sharp noise, not expecting it and her vision quickly returned to near darkened, she squeezed around his shaft again and the wave that was building overcame her. Her bladder let go and soaked her husband and their marital bed as she came hard, rasping as she struggled for breath. Stan released her and instantly she started to moan loudly. Her face was that of pain but the release she felt was far from it. Shaking, she laid Motionless as Stan removed himself from her, watching her opening resume its natural form after his girth departed. Her Lips, now swollen, shining with her juice and piss slowly closing back together.

He gave her a minute to compose herself as he stepped off of the bed to admire his wife. Quivering, she watched him watch her, and saw his still hard cock wanting more. She took a deep breath, but before she could say anything the dark expression came over him again. He grabbed her roughly by the ankles and dragged her to the edge of the bed.

“I’m not fucking done with you yet!” He told her forcefully. *Oh Fuck! I don’t know if I can take much more*! He flipped her so she laid on her stomach and dragged her legs off of the bed forcing her to bend forward and present her perfect, extremely slippery heart-shaped arse and snatch to him. With his right foot, he kicked her size 5’s apart and grabbed her makeshift pony tail again, forcing her to look straight ahead.

Holding her hair firmly, his left hand come to rest on her left hip. He pushed up and outwards revealing her to him once again. Her pussy still twitching from her last helping. He didn't need to use his hands this time but he did pin her into the side of the divan with the large muscular thighs that she loved so much. He pushed into her and she yelped and thought to herself *I can't cope with this!* His large helmet slowly pushed and pushed against the resistance. His wife yelping but helpless to do anything about it as he slid his full 9 inches into her forbidden hole. The resistance gave way at his widest point after the head.

"Argh!! It hurts"

"Good!" He liked it when it hurt her. It made him feel powerful. He withdrew and slid back into her hard but slowly. His balls slapped her wetness below. He picked the pace up.

The inside of her back hole always felt different. Almost ribbed inside, it was tighter all the way in and her very tight arsehole felt like a new cock ring running up and down his shaft.

"Oh fuck! Harder!" She whispered quickly. He needed no encouragement and released her hair, placing his and on her other hip, and watching her cheeks bounce off of him, he fucked her as hard and fast as he could. She felt her arse relax with every pass of his length, and soon enough she had no problem with him being there. The pain had been overtaken with carnal delight and he knew it.

He kept up his pace. Her arse slapping against him and him admiring it, and his heavy sacks lapping her lips and exposed clit equally well. It was too much for her again, and almost against her will, she came hard! Her voice become ing almost musical and reacting to his rhythm.

"OH...MY...GOD...I'M....CUMMING!...AAAAHHH....AAAAAAGG-GGGHHHHH.....FUUUCK.. YEEEESSSS.!!"

Her body gave out and she collapsed. He continued to abuse her back hole. She lay motionless, top half now just sprawled on the bed. The only thing keeping her up was his thighs on the back of her legs. She was quite literally, fucked.

Stan's drive was relentless. And he kept pounding, yet she had no more to give. The noise of them slapping together was deafening. *It's be funny if someone called the police!* He smiled to himself. Slap, slap, slap. He was enjoying the sound.

"Please.....babe.... I CAN'T!! Anne begged between exhausted breaths.

"I'll stop when I've finished! He told he cruelly.

"Ahhhh......ahhhhh.....ahhh!" She continued moaning.

"Tell me something dirty you'd like to do! Help me cum!""

"Ok!...well...." She had to think a little in her current state and it wasn't easy, so she could only access the part of her brain that was true, instead of making something up that Stan 'wants' to hear. She went for it.

"I want...." Slap, slap,

"To go out...." Slap slap

"And come home...." Slap slap slap

"With a.... Slap slap slap

"Strangers load in me....." slap slap slap slap

"For you to clean up!" Slap slap SLAP! Stan like what he had heard and it sent him over the edge. His balls squeezed slightly and his hot sticky load was sent deep into his wife's back passage. She felt his dick pulse as it spurted four or five times into her. He collapsed over her, still inside her.

"Pass my phone!" He told her.

She looked up and it was about a foot from her face. She hadn't even noticed it there before. She grabbed it and passed it behind her. Stan took it from her and opened his camera, and switched it to video.

"I'm recording, just so you know!"

"Urgh. Ok!"

He pointed it straight down at his still semi hard dick buried deep in his wife and clicked the red circle to record. Slowly, he pulled out, revealing his full-length inch by inch. The fact that she taken the whole thing was impressive in itself. Her hole clamped around the base of his helmet and she breathed in sharply. It felt very sensitive around him and he pulled the end out. It left her hole almost as round and open as his now evacuated piece.

"Hold yourself open!" He instructed her. She reached back and held her round ass cheeks apart for him; her pussy spread open for good measure.

"Fall onto your knees and stay open!" Again, she followed instructions as he followed, he down with the camera.

"Let it all out!" He was still clearly horny. It didn't take much for her gaping hole to release what he had deposited for her and he caught it all on camera. He stopped recording and swiped her pussy with his hand. She shuddered, being so sensitive and he knelt next to her.

Kissing her, he held her butt again.

"Come up onto the bed." She struggled to her feet and he helped her the last little bit.

"Jelly legs much?" He asked as she flopped into the wet duvet. He laid next to her.

"You really are a dirty bitch!"

“Sorry I got horny in the bath. You were very rough with me this evening!”

“Was that a problem?”

“No not at all, but I might have to wear roll necks and scarves for a week!”

“Sorry but you were too sexy, and I had to take you as I wanted!” She giggled and rested her head on his chest as before, now only shaking, covered in their mess and exhausted.

“That was incredible, I love you.”

“I love you more.” He told her and kissed her on the forehead.

Dinner Date

"We'll have the Merlot" Stan tells the pretty blonde waitress as he closes the leather-bound wine list and passes it back to her.

"No problem, sir and would you like water for the table?"

"Yes please" Anne tells her. She noticed him looking at the waitress, he always struggled to be subtle with his wandering eyes, yet she was never jealous. She accepted him for the perv he was and she loved him for it. God knows she like to look at other men and women occasionally. She walked away towards the bar, leaving them alone in the dim yet adequately lit booth. The funky exposed filament bulb hanging about a foot above their heads. Ed Sheeran was thinking out loud somewhere behind them, again.

"This song is so fucking overplayed!" He tells his wife. She ignores his musical snobbery and retorts

"She's too young for you!" Upwardly nodding in the direction, the blonde girl wiggled her hips off in

It is a nice arse to be fair. She decided internally, not that she was about to tell Stan.

"Yeah, I know, I was just noticing!"

"Oh yeah?!" She smiled at him. "Noticing what?"

"Her bra is too small, and she looks like she's about to fall out! Even you wouldn't want to miss that!"

"Very True, Mr Carter, very true." The young but extremely voluptuous waitress returned with the bottle.

"Would you like to taste?" Stan glanced at his beautiful wife with a mischievous flash. The light caught her hair a certain way and it framed her face perfectly.

“I didn’t know it was that kind of establishment” Stan remarked and winked at the waitress as she presented the bottle. Her cheeks blushed; she was clearly a little too young for his humour.

“Stan! Stop it!” Anne lightly tapped his forearm. He apologised,

“Sorry, can’t help myself. No, we don’t need to taste, thank you”. The waitress placed the bottle at the end of the table, and wiggles away from them. Both of them stopped to watch her round ass struggle to contain itself in her skinny black jeans. Stan looked back at Anne.

“I bet she’s camel toeing under that apron!” They laughed as Anne poured the wine.

As the starters came and went, they laughed and talked away, really settling into evening. Both at least one glass of wine into their night, Stan begun to feel a little merry, and as always, he started getting a little flirty with just about everyone. Anne enjoyed his humour and being a bit daft. As the waitress returned to clear the table, she thought *I hope I can laugh like this couple when I’m married*. Anne slipped a foot out of her fairly expensive heels and placed in into Stan’s crotch. She could feel his soft but meaty bulge through his dark blue jeans with her toes.

He looked across the table at his wife. No one could see her foot in the shadow. She began to gently caress his sheathed length along its side. She could feel the ridge of his helmet through the denim, knowing he was ‘commando’ just made it easier for her to tease him. He continues to stare into her eyes as she pleasures him semi-publicly. Quickly, she withdrew her foot, and the sudden look of disappointment on his face was more than apparent.

“I need a wee before the main course arrives” She shimmied out of the booth, grabbed her small clutch bag and stood at the end of the table, adjusting her figure-hugging black dress as she rose. Turning towards the direction of the toilets, she flattened the textured black skirt against her ass for her husband to watch her walk away. He did and thought to himself, *fuck I love that arse!* As he adjusts his semi through his jeans with his less visible left hand.

He sat there minding his own business for a while, phone away, as was always their rule casually watching his favourite curvy waitress, trying as always not to get caught and be outed as a pervert! She wiggled back and forth quickly between the bar and various tables and clearly enjoyed being around people. *I'll definitely give her a good tip and* he made a mental note to do so. A few more minutes passed and finally Anne arrived back at the table, catching him looking at Little Miss Blondie Curve, as she'd mentally named her.

"Enjoying the view, dirty perv?"

"Oh hey! Ha yeah kind of." He felt a small pang of embarrassment, but Anne bent down to kiss him on the cheek. She discreetly placed a finger under his nose. He knew the smell of her immediately.

Still wet, he looked over his shoulder and sucked the flavour from her finger. She returned to the booth. As her arse hit the leather on the bench, he felt his phone buzz in his pocket. Automatically he went to touch it and told himself, *Nope, no phones.*

"You ok? You took your time."

"Yeah, just had a text from Diane, she's having a few issues with Del" She made a motion with her first finger and thumb, indicating something small.

"Oh, trouble in paradise, is it?" He asked.

"Well, I don't want to give her secrets away, but let's just say that I don't think Del is maybe as at tentative as you are when it comes to satisfaction, and maybe that wouldn't be so hard if he had something to boast about"

"Ah I see, we'll I don't know what she expects from someone who drinks lager like water and will only wear a West Ham shirt! Work-shy Cunt! She'd be better off on her own, I reckon!"

"Yeah maybe!" Anne looked a little sad for her friend for a second, but her mind was soon distracted by Little Miss Blondie Curve returning with the main course.

They continued through their meal in almost silence, they both opted for the steak and it was the right choice!

"This is incredible" Stan exclaimed on more than one occasion. He decided towards the end of the course to try and use his foot on Anne.

He slipped his left foot out of his Vans classic, and still socked, he run it up the inside of Anne's smoothly shaven leg. He felt the blood rush to his dick again. He was sure that the inside of his jeans would be coated with precum, as it already felt sticky and warm against the almost rough denim.

"Uh-uhh!" Anne smirked and continued eating as if nothing had happened. The short look of disappointment rose again. He slipped his shoe back on.

"I'm gonna nip to the loo" he said quietly. Anne whispered back,

"Don't poke anyone's eye out!" And chuckled to herself.

The toilet was much brighter than the main restaurant. He unzipped himself and his considerable member flopped out by its self. The gent two urinals up was watching out of the corner of his eye, Stan heard him gasp aloud before he zipped up and left immediately.

I wonder if he was shocked, embarrassed impressed or aroused?! Stan kind of liked the idea of a guy being turned on by his cock, even though he wasn't attracted to men.

He began to pee into the urinal when he remembered that his

phone had buzzed earlier, letting go of his dick and his jeans, he dug his phone out of his left trouser pocket. The familiar message banner was covering the image of Darth Vader across his locked screen. WhatsApp, two video messages from Anne Carter.

He unlocked his phone with facial ID and tapped the green icon. Hit her name again and sure enough there was two clips. Both of which started with a still of the black dress she was currently wearing out in the restaurant. *I'd better nip into the stall*! He followed his instinct.

Lowering the volume, he hit the triangular 'play' icon floating over the image and it expanded quickly to fill his screen. He didn't need to turn the phone as Anne has kept the phone upright

The video began blandly pointing at where Anne cleavage should be, but was obscured by her lace covered black dress. The image moved out and it was clear that it had been placed on the ground, but resting against a wall or door. He could see his wife in full, but from a mouse-eye view. She stood upright and mouthed what looked like "I love you" to the camera. Slowly and seductively, she hitched the hem of her dress above the knee, taking her time to reveal the top of her black stockings. Stan had no idea she was in full kit! He presumed she was in tights and wasn't expecting anything 'extra-curricular' as they called it. The stockings merged into suspenders and then the suspender belt. A black see-through lace thong was hugging her trimmed and neat mound but with the beauty of today's technology he could easily make out the dark line of her private slit.

Still looking at the camera, she spread her legs slightly apart and begun to stroke herself with her right middle finger gently on the outside of the floral black lace panties. Once or twice, she pushed in deeper to stimulate her clit and her body gave a little shudder each time. Showing her finger to the camera, visibly wet, through her underwear, she sucked her own finger seductively and blew a kiss to camera before stepping backwards.

Stan hadn't noticed yet, as he was so engrossed in what he was watching that he'd gone hard against his jeans. He couldn't leave the cubicle yet. The door to the toilets swung open and Stan hit pause. Hard heeled steps headed to the urinal and Stan heard to gentle whoosh off a man pissing onto porcelain. Double checking the volume was off, he hit play again.

Anne was now stood directly over the toilet in the background. The wooden seat was lifted up. Stan expected her to stand and piss for him. But he was surprised. As she winked again seductively at the camera, she began to piss gently at first, through the delicate material of her sexy laced panties. The material kept the stream steady as she increased her flow. Mid way through, Anne grabber the waistband of her knickers and pulled up forming a black, sopping wet camel toe. She stepped towards the camera until her face could be seen in frame, and she squatted to show her husband what she'd done. Her left hand came into shot to rub her wet pussy through the lace, her wedding ring glinting as she did. The video stopped and shrank back down.

The pisser clicked his heels towards the sink and as the water gushed, Stan clicked the next play triangle. Starting again in the centre of her chest, the camera pans out again quickly, this time showing her still hitched dress and panties. She stood up and ran her thumbs around the inside of the waistband again. Sliding her right finger down the front side of the panties, revealing her neatly trimmed lips. The knickers distorted it more and gave a a bit of a front wedgie. She ignored it and stood over the camera again. Leaning forward to show her face, she sucked her middle two fingers slowly, wetting them and stood quickly. Holding herself open with her left hand she immediately shoved them inside her own wetness. She clearly enjoyed it, her body gave a little shudder once again and she fingered herself hard and fast for about ten seconds, forcing her delicate fingers back and forth inside herself. She stopped and returned to face the camera licking her fingers clean again. Now Stan knew where the familiar scent under his nose came from now.

Standing up she turned around to show her husband her round ass, the discreet bumps of her skin showing in the harsh fluorescent light. She bent forward revealing the covered mound between her legs and slowly begun to remove the lace panties. They reached the bottom of her ass and the Stan could see the pussy and arsehole that he knew and loved so well, she stopped to spread herself, again revealing Stan's secret little skin tag that he loves so much on her. She released her cheeks and stood up, allowing the panties to fall to the floor. She turned around closed the toilet lid and sat on it.

Opening her legs to once again to reveal what Stan always considered as her very tidy quim. Holding her soaked panties up to the camera, she delicately folded them in half left to right, and the Again, creating a neat little rectangle of lace material. She the rolled it from the top down. *What's she doing?* Stan mused. It was soon very clear. Between her left first and middle fingers, she opened her cunt as wide as she could (without help of course) and begun to insert one end of the rolled-up panties into herself like a dildo. *Oh my god, I think I'm gonna blow in my jeans!* He thought, knowing that this woman is sat in the next room casually finishing her steak.

It didn't take long for the whole material dildo to disappear into her accommodating snatch. She laid back on the toilet slight and. Continued to masturbate slowly. The very tip of the black insertion just protruding out of her. She stopped what she was doing before she climaxed and stood up.

Still recording, placing the phone down, she pulled the hem of her skirt down and made herself look presentable, flipping the camera, she showed herself off in the mirror, briefly cupping her breasts for her intimate audience, and opened the door to the main restaurant. As she stepped out, the video stopped.

Holy shit! Stan thought. *What a dirty bitch my wife is, sitting there with lacy panties inside her. Fuck I've been a while!*

He sent a quick text to Anne

> Sorry babe, I got your texts obviously and had to watch them in the cubicle. I'll be out shortly. Xx

She replied

> You better not have had a wank in there! Xx
>
> .....
>
> I haven't, but it's a little obvious that I enjoyed them. 2 secs! Xx
>
> .....
>
> Ok my love xxxxx

It took everything he had to get rid of his hard on but the more he tried, the more he couldn't stop seeing his wife putting her own underwear inside herself. In the end, he untucked his shirt and used the teenage boys trick of tucking the end in his waist band, he skipped washing his hands without thinking, and headed back to the table.

“Are you alright my love? You seem a little flustered!” Anne quizzed as Little Miss Blondie Curve head to the table.

“Oops! Your friend is heading our way!”

“Was everything ok for you guys? She asked the pair.

“Everything was just perfect actually, thank you!” He looked knowingly over at his wife. Although his blood was up, he had a sudden wave of overwhelming love for her hit him as the light caught her perfectly symmetrical face just right. She caught his glance, and even after all these years it still made her blush. Little Miss Blondie Curve picked up on their mood too, and cleared the plates quickly and quietly. Before she left, she interrupted,

“Would you like to see the dessert menu at all?”

“Oh, not for me” Stan told her, and Anne shook her head.

“I’ll have a coffee liqueur though please” she said.

“Of course, and for you, sir?”

“Pint of Peroni please.”

“Of course!” she turns on her heel with the plates and left them in relative piece.

“A bit full are you, my love?” Stan asked his wife. She smiled at him knowingly.

“You could say that. But I tell you what though!”

“What?” He asked quickly.

“Give me your hand!” She grabbed his wrist under the table and forced it between her legs. He nearly hit his chin on the table. As he discreetly felt between her legs, she whispered

“I’m so fucking wet!”

“You are n’all! So, what’s the plan after this then? It’s only 8.30!”

“I don’t know, I’m undecided, but it’s. Long walk home.”

A short while later, Stan holds the door open for his wife and she steps through in her red coat over her black lace, he follows her wearing a black North Face over his shirt. They join hands, her walking on the left and begin to stroll along the empty High Street.

"How does it feel walking with your knickers on the inside then?" Anne laughed

"It feels really fucking sexy, but I think they are starting to absorb my wetness. I might have to remove them soon!"

Oh, that's disappointing, but if it's not comfortable then you probably should. With that Stan cut away to the left in front of Anne, and quickly led her into a dark side alley. He pushed her against the rough brick, and she felt it snag in the material of her coat as he kissed her softly, yet forcefully. She felt her pussy start to open slightly and her clit throb. Stan reached between his wife's legs and slowly moved his hand up to her wet, aching twat.

"Can you keep them in for five minutes? He asked her in a low voice?

"I'm sure I can manage" good he told her as his strong finger delicately circled her clit amidst the cool night air. He sucked his finger to indicate he was finished and pulled her by the hand back out of the alleyway, careful to avoid bringing attention to themselves as they stepped into the light.

"I've had fun on our date night so far my love!" Anne told Stan, he released her hand and placed his arm around her waist as they walked.

"Me too" he told her contently as he kissed her cheek. She smiled at him and felt the usual twinge down below.

They stopped on the corner Recreation Street. The October evening air beginning to cool enough to cause their breath to fog.

"Do you want to walk up and round the street or cut over the Rec?" Stan asked her

"I don't mind, I'm happy walking for a bit if you are."

"Of course, let's go over the Rec then." They started to walk on the narrow tarmac path and drift away from the orange hue of the street lights. Stan slid his now cool hand up the back of Anne's leg.

"Oh, that's cold!" She exclaimed.

"I know" he didn't stop. After a few more paces, an idea struck him!

"Stand there!" She stopped as he walked a few yards back. He pulled his phone from his pocket.

"Show me your arse!" She smiled at him silently, turned around and did as instructed.

CLICK the phone camera sound went!

"Oi! Cheeky!"

"What? I want to take pictures of my wife! Now get your tits out!"

"No way it's too cold!"

"Exactly, your nipples will be hard.!" She unbuttoned her dress and pulled the bra down over her tits exposing them to the night air, and Stand camera.

"Now show me your cunt!"

"Stanley! Language! You know I prefer it when you call it my dirty cunt!!"

"Sorry my love, show me your dirty cunt then!" She hitches her skirt exposing her still stuffed pussy; the cold breeze feels oddly satisfying over it. Stan let's put a short chuckle.

"Hot!"

“Get him out then!”

“What?” He asks

“Get your cock out!” Come on!” He unbuttons his trousers and unzips his fly. It falls out by itself as always. She walks towards him, skirt still up and sees him rise and grow in the darkness.

“She kisses him and takes his large dick in her hand and begins to slowly pump it next to her. He returns the favour by placing his hand between her legs and circling her clit once again. They stand in the darkness, fog closing in kissing passionately, and gentling fondling each other for a few minutes, when Stan pulls away.

“Come on!” He leads her away swiftly, her naked white arse glowing against the darkness, pussy beginning to moisten again, despite her plug and his hard cock still swaying as he moved. A Few yards later, they come across a galvanised steel gates the fog with rounded hoops at the waist high top. Anne knows this place; she’s spent many an afternoon here with the kids.

They move quickly through the gate and it squeaks conspicuously against the almost deafening silence.

“Shhh!” Anne giggles! He pulls her over to the climbing frame and lifts her up on to the first level about gate height.

“Whoa!” She tries to be quiet but felt like she was going to go over the other side! The cold metal startles her too! Stan pushes her back hard with an almost savage rage and whips her legs apart exposing her juice pussy the night sky. Like a possessed animal, his head dives between her legs and lick her trimmed outer lips. His wife’s familiar pussy glistening underneath strange moonlight she lays back to receive his service and gently holds his head.

He zones in on her clit, it’s throbbing against the cold air and his mouth feels especially hot in comparison. He kisses her trimmed pussy all around her stuffed entrance and gently tugs her panties still filling her hole. It felt tight and it resisted against his pulls. She gasped at the new sensation. Gently with his teeth his kept tugging while rubbing her clit with his tongue. She started to feel the familiar rise from within. She told him,

“Keep… tugging…. I’m going to…. cum!” Stan increased the frequency of the light tugs and the speed of his thumb. She started to moan!

“Oh my god!” She tried to be quiet but it came out anyway,

“Fuuuucckk!” She panted heavily across her groans. Stan stopped and kissed her pussy lips. One each side.

“Enjoy that?” Yes, help me down.

Her legs were jelly, his cock was hard and dripping with clear precum, she could see it reflecting against the darkness. She knew he needed to be finished.

“Where do you want me?”

“Bend over the net swing!”she staggered over to it, holding her dress up still, but starting to feel the cold. The swing hung off of 4 long ropes connected to a pivot at the top, and was about a meter round converted in cargo net. She bent over it grasping the padded edge, and presented herself to her husband. He came up behind her and placed his hands on that perfect white arse, separating her cheeks slightly, and lined his purple head up with her now empty and satisfied clam.

“Fuck me hard!” She begged in a delicate voice. He held her hips and forces his huge, hard penis all the way into her. She gasped with surprise. Even after all this time his size still shocks her occasionally and this was one of those times. He withdrew slowly, and rammed her fast once again.

She pushed back against his massive length and they began their familiar carnal rhythm. Stan heard the gate squeak.

He continued to Pound his wife as he looked over his shoulder and saw a lone figure edging slowly towards them. *What the fuck? Should we stop?* Anne was none the wiser and still being obliviously fucked hard. Stan didn't stop. The stranger stopped just out of reach of them and slightly behind. Stan continued to look at him. *Maybe he wants to join in.* Stan was never going to allow that to happen. He held a hand up to him as if the say

"What?" The guy showed him both palm in a non-threatening demeanour and pointed to his eyes and cock. Stan knew immediately what he wanted and gestured the ok sign to him.

Stan withdrew from his wife slowly, allowing the stranger to get a good look at her used, married cunt. Slowly, he dipped himself back into her and out again ensuring his new friend had the best possible view. The friend unzipped his trousers quietly and took out his own cock. Not small but not like Stan's monster. It was already hard and Stan turned his attention back to his good lady.

He rammed his hard dick back into her, deeper and harder, the swing was helping him force his way into he as she bent forward and away from him. The stranger's hand was getting faster and faster too. Watching that impressive penis disappearing into her smooth shiny wet cunt.

Stan pulled her into him holding her by the shoulders, his dick filling her cavity entirely and whispered into her ear.

"Don't react, and don't freak out, but we're being watched and have been for a couple of minutes. He's behind me wanking over you."

Anne's eyes widened with a bit of panic on the darkness, but he felt her dampen once more

"I'm allowing him to stay is that okay?"

"Yes, let me turn over so he can see!" He pulled out of her quickly and turned to the stranger.

"Come closer, she wants you to watch.

She laid back across the swing thinking *who knew the playground could be such fun?* Shuffling so her ass was at the edge for her husband to access her, she unbuttoned the dress again and took her tits out once more. Nipples hardening more against the night air. She spoke to the man.

"Come closer, it ok!" He stepped over and couldn't help but admire her wonderful breasts.

Stan took his wife by the ankles and opens her legs. She reached down and opened her slit wider for him and begun playing with her clit for the umpteenth time this evening. Stan filled her again slowly for his audience then began to fuck her harder and harder until it was so hard the stranger thought he might have to look away.

Anne was stifling vocalisation as best she could and finding it incredibly difficult. The stranger was wanking near her right shoulder, and she kept looking at him and her husband. She loved seeing this new dick take some pleasure from her, the friend started to breath heavy.

"Don't you dare waste that! Put it on me!" The stranger stepped closer to her, now stroking his cock directly over her, his dick almost brushing her nipple as her husband continues to plough relentlessly. The strangers knees buckled and his load escaped him violently. It shot straight across her nipple and she immediately felt the hotness on her cold skin, all the way down her stomach and over her mound, some even hitting Stan in the pubes.

"Oh my god!" Anne's rush was coming on again! "COME ON!..... HARDER...... HARDER......COME ON!......FILL ME UP.......FILL UP MY CUNT! As she held herself open! She came again, clamping her vaginal muscles around Stan's girth once again. And moaned in a high pitch. Stan let go to and his body tensed as he fired a gigantic load into his wife's twitching pussy. The stranger backed away.

“No need to rush off!” Stan said. Did you enjoy her? Shyly, the street replied.

“You’ve no idea! It’s made my year I think. Are you married?”

“Yes this is my wife, my very sexy wife” Stan grinned. Anne was laying with her still dress up, tits out and legs open on the swing. Her husbands load was watering down and running out of her pulsation quim. She waved at him!

“Hi!” As she giggled a little.Stan told him,

“Feel free to get a good look before you head off, we’re in no hurry!”

“Are you sure?” The stranger asked the question more to Anne than Stan. So she answered.

“A few minutes won’t hurt.” As she put her hands behind her head. Her husband came behind due her and kissed her as the stranger took his place between her legs to observe her from a new perspective.

“I know I maybe speaking out of turn here,” the stranger said, “but you have a beautiful cunt!”

“I’ve been telling her that for year!” Stan told him. The stranger continued.

“I’m sorry to ask, but may I touch?” He was careful not to direct the question at either one of them. Anne looked at her husband and shrugged as if to say “I don’t mind” Stan mimicked her and said, “sure just for a minute.”

The stranger wasted no time. His warm hand fell onto Anne’s covered belly and moved immediately up to her exposed breasts. He felt nice on her, they were warm and soft. He run his hand down to her thighs and moved them in towards her messy pussy. He leaned in to smell it.

“I’d love to clean it for you!”

“What do you mean?” Stan asked.

"To lick all the mess up and clean her" he said a little sheepishly.

"Oh?! Oh, I see. Babe, what do you think?" She laughed.

"If you're happy, it saves me a job!" Stan gave him a nod and for the first time watch another man lick his wife's pretty little pussy.

The stranger licked her outer lips from bottom to top, First left then right. Then he moved inwards and worked both sides of her crease, finishing by tongue ing the middle of her slit, from the bottom of her married hole, slowly to her very sensitive clit. She winced and giggled as his tongue hit it. Finally, he asked her to sit a little, allowing the last of Stan's load to fall out of her. The stranger willingly took it and swallowed it, giving her a final lick for good measure, he gently kissed her lady lips, and spoke

"All done madam! Thank you for allowing me to meet you this evening, it's truly made my day!"

With that he stood up, zipped his trousers and disappeared into the fog. The gate squeaked as he left the play area.

Anna sat up in the swing, her exposed cunt still damps from their new friend efforts, and turned to Stan.

"Are you ok? God that was sexy! We're you ok with another man there?"

"Put it this way babe, I'm hard again already, and when we get home, you won't be walking tomorrow!" She straightened her attire and hair as best she could. They held hand and walked out of the squeaky gate.

"Is that so, mr Carter?"

Drive

“I’m glad they finally managed to tie the knot” Anne said as she scrolled through the pictures on her phone.

“Yeah, they looked great together, and I hope they make it. I mean, I think we’re lucky to have what we have but I just don’t imagine too many people being as close as we are!” Stan replied as he indicated to overtake Eddie Stobarts ‘Fiona’. The BMW mad light work of it as he cruised up to 86mph without thinking.

“Do you remember our wedding?” She asked Still scrolling, quickly past the dick pic she’d been sent randomly by an ex-client. It had saved to her camera roll and she hadn’t thought to delete it.

“Do I? Ha! I still have wanks about our wedding night! You were stunning and every time I looked at you that day, I thought you were too beautiful for me. Then at the same time I couldn’t wait to get you to the suite! Don’t get me started!”

“Surely you can’t remember all that?” She mused

“You wanna bet?”

“That’s impressive Mr Carter, and a little bit sexy. So, tell me, what else do you think about while you wank?”

“Well, usually you, and the stuff we have done.”

“But don’t you imagine things? Have fantasies?” She probed him further.

“Well, not really I don’t think. I think we have a good sex life and we do what we want when we fancy it. How about you? What do you play to?” She blushed a little at being asked.

“Well, you know, whatever I’m thinking about, like you mainly stuff we’ve done.”

“Oh, so I should have fantasies but you don’t necessarily have them either? He chuckled and she smiled at him cheekily.

“I never said that!” She retorted.

“Go on then, tell me a fantasy of yours” he demanded lightly.

“Uh uh! If you want to know mine, Mr Carter, you better tell me yours first!”

“Hmm hard ball is it Mrs Wife? Ok give me a minute.

A few miles passed in silence. Not awkward but each of them really taking the time to decide what fantasy they were going to share. He was deciding whether or not to make one up and tell her what she wants or to tell the truth, she was thinking about all the things they had done, and wondering what there was left to do.

“I have two fantasies” Stan told her nervously and she noticed.

“Are you nervous?”

“No! Well, a bit.”

“Stan Carter, we’ve been married 15 years, you’ve eaten fruit out of me, I’ve masturbated in the back of a taxi for you, and that’s just the tip of it all, do you really think I’ll judge you?

“You might think I’m weird!”

“You are, but we’re married to each other and both pretty kinky, so it’s not really gonna be a big deal.”

“Only if you’re sure, AND you’re gonna tell me yours!”

“I will, I promise. A few more minutes pass, he breathes through his nerves.

“Ok, here goes, number one!!” He says matter of factly

“Go on”

"Well, please don't hate me, but I have developed a bit of an unhealthy curiosity to your friend Diane." He glanced sideways at her, she was calm and unchanged. *Oh god what am I doing.* He thought.

"Right? So, you want to fuck her? That's just a crush, not a fantasy!"

"Actually no, I've got no intention of fucking her or wanting to for that matter. I actually just like to look at her. If I'm really honest, I'd get a kick out of watching her, without her knowing. Maybe undressing or showering, or even masturbating and fucking. But I don't want to touch her.

"I see, so you want to be a voyeur?

"And how would you watch her?"

"Well, I don't know. Maybe if she stayed with us, a peep hole or a tiny camera? I don't know. It's stupid anyway. Forget about it."

"Stan, it's ok. I'm your wife and we should be able to talk about this stuff. Be specific I promise it's ok!"

"Well, my specific fantasy, I suppose, is that she would stay with us, for whatever reason; and maybe leave the door open a crack as she changes. I'd like to wank and watch. I'd also like similar for the shower too. But ultimately, I'd like to see the two of you share a bottle of wine and get cosy with each other. I want to watch you eat each other's other pussies, that sort of thing."

"It's actually pretty hot to hear you say that you know. Especially that you're not interested in touching etc. And how would we arrange it?

"Well, honestly I don't know, it'd have to be you luring her in somehow. Sounds a bit too predatory for me though."

"Maybe, who knows. Might be a workable fantasy. No harm no foul and stuff! What would you say if I could lay my hands on naughty pictures of her for you as an interim? She felt her little tingle below at the thought of her husband watching her friend.

"What? How?"

"Us women discuss all sorts, I'm sure I could drop something in. Not about you obviously." She laughed as she spoke and continued.

"I'll even wank with you over them, how's that sound?"

"Oh my god, so hot! Look what you've done to my dick!"

"That's not difficult my love!"

"True, so come on, tell me yours!"

"But you said you had two?"

"Yes, well it's one for one, isn't it?"

"Okay then." She said with an heir of superiority.

"I briefly told you this when you made me ruin the bedsheets the other week, I don't know if you heard."

"Hmm, doesn't ring any bells, but go on." His cock throbbing inside his wranglers.

"Well, bearing in mind this is a fantasy, but I'd like to go out one evening to a bar, by myself. I'd sit at the bar sipping a drink and wait for men to come and buy me a drink, try and flirt with me. I'd flirt back of course, and for the right guy, I'd let him touch me." She looked hard at her husband and raised her hands to her tits; she squeezed gently. It felt nice.

"He could touch me where he liked." She paused. She could see his dick on the left side of his wranglers bulging now.

"Uh huh!" He was trying hard to listen and concentrate on the road while imagining what she was saying.

"Then, he would take me somewhere. Somewhere naughty hopefully like his car or an alleyway, and I'd allow him to do as he wanted with me. There would be no limits to his depravity. And I'd be complicit." His left hand rested on his cock through the denim.

"Afterwards, I'd dress myself up, respectably again and come home to you. I'd show you what he'd left inside me and ask you to clean it up. In my head you would and then we'd have more mind-blowing sex." She looked nervously, sideways at him and awaited his response. Vocalising her own fantasy had tuned her on and she was getting a little damp in the right places.

"To be fair, it does sound hot. And actually, it Segway's me into my second fantasy, as if by design!" He laughed.

"Oh, does it? Now this is getting interesting, husband!" She had the dirty look on her face that he loved so much. His nerves had left now and he was once again calm.

"So, in short, I want to watch you with another man." He fell silent and awaited a response.

"That's it? You need to be a little more descriptive, I'm getting a bit wet over here!" She began to rummage in her handbag.

"Ah ha! Got it!"

"What?"

"Drive and talk, Carter.!"

"Well specifically, I've been enjoying the idea of being humiliated by you." She unbuttoned her black trousers, unclicked her seatbelt and slid them down to her feet, and fastened her seatbelt again. Stan was surprised to see her with no panties on.

"Commando babe?"

"Forgot to pack extras. Carry on!"

"Well, I want to have you invite someone over. Could be a friend or colleague, or just a stranger. I'd maybe be tied to a chair or hand cuffed or blindfolded. That would be up to you. But you'd be in control." She sat with her legs together, naked from the waist down.

"You'd invite them in. Maybe we can get one of those metal cock cages like on the bondage porn. But whatever, you invite him in. You introduce him to me, tell him things like, he doesn't bother pleasuring me, or I need a bigger man or younger or whatever. You get the idea."

"Yeah, I think so" she reached between her legs and placed whatever she got out of her bag down there.

"What is that?"

"Emergency vibrator. Bullet. it's always in my bag!"

"Oh well, you never know! Yeah, so, anyway, you'd humiliate me verbally like that, and you make me watch you pleasure him, and make me watch him pleasuring you. But I'd want you to truly enjoy it. It wouldn't work unless you did."

Anne was now laid back into her chair, with her little gadget buzzing away, and starting the wriggle into the feel of it. Her hips begun to rock slightly.

"So, let me get this straight, your fantasy is to give me free reign to invite a stud over, tie you up, and humiliate you by fucking Him in front of you? Oh god, that's hot!"

The vibrator was working it charm on Stan's wife.

"Lorry coming up!"

"Hmm, slow down a bit see if he notices!" She told him.

"Oh, you are horny today, aren't you?"

"A bit" she replied playfully.

Stan slowed the car to 60 as they approached the red and white artic. Anne laid her seat back a touch and got her tits out too, for good measure. Stan hovered by the truck's driver door for a bit. Hoping the driver had noticed; he had no way of seeing up. His dick now throbbing and restricted while his wife sat naked freely next to him. He sped back up to a reasonable speed and the truck flashed his lights several times in quick succession.

"I think he's thanking us; he's flashing he told Anne"

"Hmmmm" she moaned satisfactorily with her eyes closed and

hands between her legs.

“Open your mouth!” She told her husband. She stuck two very slimy fingers in and his tongue took every drop from her.

“So come on then, horny bitch! Tell me another one!”

“Oooh fuck I’d better stop for a minute! Okay!” She turned to him and unbuttoned his jeans, eagerly, she pulled out her man's big cock and it stood upright. He had to shuffle his jeans down a little for it to be comfortable. Wrapping a hand around it she said four words

“I want a gangbang!”

“How many?” No hesitation in him at all

“I’m not sure, 4 or 5 probably.”

“Well don’t hold back on me know you’ve got him out!”

“Well, I imagine it’s a special occasion; something like birthday or anniversary and we go to a hotel for a weekend. You blindfold me and lay me on the bed. I hear the door and I hear soft feet in the carpet. And one voice, yours, saying “help yourselves gents” or something like that. then I’d be surrounded by these guys, unable to see and cocks being stuffed everywhere and hands everywhere. Oh god it just sounds amazing, doesn’t it?”

“I suppose, and where would I be?”

“That’s up to you, watch or join in? Both?

“Yeah, I’d probably watch and film it. You know I love you being my little personal porn star. So where would they cum?

“Wherever they’d like, but I would like to experience lots of guys cumming in me.”

“That’s disgusting! I fucking love it! Cock hungry little wife that you are! She unbuckled her seatbelt and knelt up in her seat. The car disapproved, but Stan chose to ignore it.

“So, my husband approves, does he? Glancing down at his exposed cock, he tells her

"It would appear so!" Then carefully, so as not to jolt him while driving she leaned forward and took his cock in her mouth. He leaned back and let out a groan and tried to keep his eyes firmly affixed to the road.

Anne's naked behind was now in full display of the passenger car window. Her plump pussy very nearly pushed up against the glass.

"Another lorry coming up!" He warned her, but she chose to ignore him by concentrating on her mid-journey snack. He decided to slow down to 60 again. This time he had a good look up at the driver before pulling alongside. He saw him glance in his mirror. Bringing the window level and matching the Lorry's speed, Anne continued to suck. Both hands around her husband's dick and her head bouncing away.

"We're level." He told her. She begun to sway her round exposed arse left and right slowly. She parted her legs as best she could to show the driver her shaven clam and reached between her legs.

With her first and third finger, she spread her lips a little, ensuring the best possible view as her middle finger pressed gently on her now pulsing clit. She started to pleasure herself again, manually this time.

She was becoming very horny very quickly and started to make the usual noises but his wife masturbating for a trucker was so hot for him, that he couldn't help himself. It sent Stan's blood rushing and out of nowhere, his balls did their usual tighten and his loins released his seed into his wife's mouth.

"Oh fuuuuck!" He exclaimed. She was startled by it, but it was no big deal. She allowed him to pulse into her mouth, his hot load hitting the back of her throat. She started to swallow as she continued to suck more gently now. Stan's legs were shaking, and it took all his effort to stay in a straight line. She allowed some of his mess to dribble down his shaft. He could feel it, but Anne soon took care of it. With her still cummy tongue, she licked his shaft all the way from base to tip. Momentarily forgetting she was being watch by another driver and they were both in moving vehicles.

She allowed Stan's softening cock to relax. He was spent already, and she knew it. As she knelt up, she kissed him on the lips. He always loved to taste cock on her mouth. She remembered the lorry driver.

"Oh, we're still being watched!" She sounded surprised.

"We'll I enjoyed the show." Stan said as he put his foot down again. As he sped off the lorry sounded his large horn and flashed his lights as Anne made her way back into her seat.

"I think he did too!" She said as she laughed. She placed both of her Feet on the dash and spread her legs.

"Well, I'm not finished yet!" she told him dryly.

Stan looked at her with a smile and nodded gently.

"Go on then!" She turned slightly in her seat and tuned in the back footwell with her right arm.

"That'll do!" She pulled round an empty Diet Coke bottle for their last service stop.

"Need a piss?"

"No" she told him quietly as she retrieved her little bullet for the cup holder in which she'd left it.

"I need something in me!"

Spreading herself, she needed no extra lubrication. She was extremely wet, and placing the bobbled base of the bottle at her entrance she begun to push one corner inside of herself. It took a little persuasion, but after 30 seconds or so, she'd relaxed her internal muscles enough to grant the bottle permission to enter. Stan was trying to watch as best he could. She breathed out a long deep breath, as the widest part of the bottle approached her tight spot. With her left hand, she clicked the bullet on with her thumb and it buzzed in her hand. Placing onto her clit, she gasped sharply; It momentarily allowed the hips of the bottle to pass into her and she pushed it in up to the label.

Stan had girth, and she knew what a lucky girl she was to have such a big dick to call on anytime she wanted but this stretched like she hadn't been stretched in a long time. It felt extremely tight and she felt very very full. The bullet made short work of her intentions and like Stan, without warning she also felt her normal rush jump on her quickly.

"Oh GOD!" She shouted in a higher pitch than usual as her pussy clamped tight around the clear bottle and pulsed quickly. Her legs squeezed together automatically, and Stan reached over and squeezed her right breast as she climaxed in his new BMW. She collapsed into the leather bucket seat for a moment, closed her eyes and breathed deeply.

The bullet was still buzzing in her palm, and she clicked it off with her thumb unconsciously. Laying sprawled out, with the clear plastic bottle still inside her, she dropped her feet onto the grey carpeted mat.

"Did you enjoy that my love?" Her husband asked her. She sighed as she spoke.

"Huh! Yes, I did! Very much so!" She reached down to remover the bottle.

"That's fucking hot you know!"

"It's big! Maybe we're have to get a nice big dildo, it's been a long time since my pussy felt that full!"

"That's not a bad idea!" Stan agreed as she slowly removed it.

"I need a wee babe; can we stop at the next services?"

"That depends, are you staying like that to pee or dressing?"

"Well, I was going to dress!"

"Services it is then, there's a parking spot just up here, if you want to just squat and go!"

"Hmm that sounds ok, let's do that!"

A mile or so along, Stan pulled in. It was dark, and late. He got out of the car first, careful to switch off the interior light. He came round to her side a whipped his large dick out and started to kiss at the edge of the grassy area. He shook and zipped up. Opening the car door, he held his hand out to invite his newly naked wife out into the night air. It was cool and instantly she got goosebumps. Her nipples hardened against the breeze.

"It's fucking freezing! Whose idea was this?" She said as Stan fished his phone out of his pocket.

"Hang on!" He said as he opened the camera.

"Are you filming?"

"Of course. Right, go then!" the light on her phone illuminated his wife against the blackness, with a hint of metallic grey paintwork.

Anne opened her legs and squatted half way, her butt sticking out, and release her bladder. Her legs were still wobbly from the coke bottle incident, but she started to trickle none the less. Stan was wearing his dirty look.

Her stream increased in speed and pressure and it started to spatter the inside of her legs. It was a clear straw colour against the torchlight, and puddle with a froth on the stoney lay-by at her feet.

Slowing to a trickle, she stood a little higher.

"I've got no loo roll!"

"Sit on the bonnet!" Stan instructed.

The metal was warm under her cold bottom, and Stan handed her the phone.

"Keep filming!" He instructed. She slid her naked behind up onto the new bonnet, and spread her Legs wide. Pointing the camera, her husband dutifully begun to clean her wet mess. He knew he was weird for liking it, but between them it never mattered. He loved it when she pissed for him, and sometimes she would randomly send him video of her in the courthouse or the office toilets.

He took every drop on and kissed her delicately, and finally took a little suck if her clit. A large lorry whizzed passed them, headlights creeping up quickly and gave them a honk of the horn!

"I think it's one of our friends from earlier! Must recognise the motor!" They both laughed, his head inched from her mound.

In the distance, Stan caught a glimpse of flashing blue.

"I think we'd better get in the car before we end up on a list!"

"Good idea!"

They both had just closed the door as two police cars passed them at speed, light going wild and they laughed!

"Close call, husband! You're gonna get me struck off one day!"

Stan smiled and looked at her lovingly, even though she was still naked, worn out and a bit slimy below.

"Nah, not if it's just me and you! And it always will be. Now get dressed you pissy little whore wife, someone might see you naked! Love you!"

"I love you too." They kissed as Stan fired up the 5 series.

Massage

"Make sure you're home in good time today!"

"I'm on my way now" Stan tells his wife as he pulls out of the road adjoining his office. The full click of his indicators interjecting their conversation. He continues,

"Why, what's occurring?" In his mock Welsh accent.

"Just get home by six!" Anne tells him cheekily. He can hear in her voice that something is afoot, she'll never divulge before time and he knows better than to push.

"Okay, are the kids alright?"

"Yeah, they're staying at mums for the weekend, she's just collected them"

"Oh, I see!" Now he knows that the something afoot is about to get interesting. *A child free surprise on a Friday night.* He feels a small twinge in his cock.

The drive home was uneventful, and Stan had slipped into the usual commuters' hypnosis. If you were to ask him about the journey, he wouldn't be able to tell you. The weather was dreary and autumnal; grey skies and reddish browns in the trees. The rain slowly drizzling small spots onto the windscreen before the Beamer's wipers automatically clears them to the side. It was dark before he arrived home. As he pulls into the driveway, the left tyre dips into the water filled pothole before rolling onto the gravel driveway. The security light pops into life, highlighting him against the black leather seats surrounded by a sea of pearlescent blue paintwork. The side door of the house opens as he climbs stiffly out of the car.

"Hello, husband. How was the drive? Do you want tea?"

"Hello wife, yes please and it was ok, traffic was a bit shit leaving town, but other than that it was alright. Why have I been relegated to the tradesman's entrance?

"Just go straight to the bathroom and have a shower, I'll bring your tea up".

"Er, right ok!" *This is weird* he thinks to himself as he kicked his black leather shoes into the corner.

He takes his time in the shower, it's been a long day and he would much rather have not gone into the office this morning.

Facing the black marble tiles, he hangs his head and allows the hot water to run down and around his face, the heat and pressure feel comforting as he supports himself with his hands on the wall.

The bathroom door swings open fully as Anne kicks it gently with her slippered foot from under her fluffy grey robe and places the blue 'best dad ever' mug on black marble sink unit.

"Tea"

"Thanks babe, so what's happening then?"

"Once you've showered. There will be something for you to wear on the bed, go put it on"

"Hmm ok" he replied curiously, sweeping the wet hair backwards from his face. Anne stood there admiring him for just a second longer. His body isn't as athletic as maybe it once was, but she loved his broad shoulders and his chest as she always had. And his thighs, no matter how his body had changed Over the years, his thighs had always remained the same and that dick of course!

Stan stepped out of the shower and dried himself off. Never fully though, which always made Anne cringe a little. With droplets still adorning his shoulders, he walked through to the bedroom, where oddly, the lights were off. He flicked them on. Nothing really out of the ordinary here save for a large white folded towel on the tartan bedspread and a note, hand written 'Stan' on the outside. It was quite obviously Anne's handwriting. Down stairs, Anne was waiting at the bottom step listening, waiting for him to cross the landing into the bedroom. Stan sat on the bed, naked with his considerable member hanging between his legs and began to read.

My darling husband,

I'm sorry that you had to work on your birthday, I know you hate it when you have to.

Tonight, I want to be focussed on you, I have arranged a little something for you, I need you to trust me, relax and go along with it.

When you have finished reading this note, make your way to the dining room, where you will find a massage table. Lay on it face down, and call out "READY" when you're are in place.

Enjoy yourself, and Happy birthday,

Your loving wife, Anne

Xxx

Well, this could be interesting, she does do a great massage, and I hope she sucks me off! Surely, she will for my birthday! His cock started to pulse a little, the vein across the top started to poke its way out and his ball sack begun to tighten gently. He wrapped the towel around his waist and tucked it as he always did. The bulge of his semi hardness showing through.

Downstairs, Anne heard the bedroom door open and skulked silently into the living room to make her final preparations.

Stan reached the bottom of the stairs, and turned immediately right into the dining room. The light was dim, only barely lit by four real candles. *Ha! Four candles!!* He thought as he chuckled to himself.

The massage table that had replaced their regular antique table and chairs looked new and sturdy.

Metal framed with black leather covering. Topped with soft fluffy white towels. The face hole pushed through slightly. *Needs a cock hole!* He lay on the bench, placed his hands by his side, his face in the hole and called.

"Ready"

He heard the door swish over the thick grey carpet, and in the dim light he could make out a pair of feet, bare save for black nylon tights over them appear below his face hole.

Oh yes! She's got the full kit on tonight, she must be horny! He thought he heard the subtle squeak of someone sitting in the leather chair in the corner, but decided he'd imagined it. He could see Anne's feet below him.

Relaxing, he began to breath deeply as the lightly scented oils were rubbed into his shoulders. The small hands spread the oil with expertise across his large back, and as the hand slid gently down his spine, increasing in pressure with each pass, he could feel the swell of her lace covered breast lightly scratch his skin. He never minded tits touching him! The hand continued slowly, yet firmly. Arms, then hands. He felt the towel being lifted and placed carefully on his arse, exposing his upper thigh.

Why is she bothering with a towel? He pondered. The massage continued to complete the back of his legs to his feet. Anne's familiar voice told him,

"Turn yourself over and keep your eyes closed." He obliged.

His now hard dick swayed against the soft cotton of the lifted towel leaving a sticky trail of Precum. It's full 9" length brimming with hot blood, making his circumcised purple dome shine softly in the candle light. The towel now draped back over his modesty, pithed like a steeply angled tent over his stomach. The warm oil starts to be rubbed into his large barrel chest. Small familiar hands working their magic. They work again, chest stomach, sides, arms. The towel is lifted and the massage of his leg begins. Slowly, firmly from top to bottom, always one hand in contact with his skin. The second leg begun; the oily little finger accidentally glances against the side of his tight scrotum as she runs her smooth hand across the top of his thigh. He lets out a small shudder and a smile. The hand continues to gently work his legs and he feels suitably relaxed.

He feels the hands lift away from him. *That was incredible.* He lets out a sigh, and as he does, he feels the cool air rush in where his towel is lifted away and before he can react, is placed over his face.

"What the?" He exclaims muffled through the thick towel. Anne's voice responds calmly.

"Relax and trust me". He relaxes back again as his hand is guided onto the lace thonged ass he's so familiar with. He strikes it gently. *Has she lost weight? I've told her not to! I love that arse as it is!*

A delicate hand grabs the base of his veiny shaft, half cupping his balls at the same time, the opposite end of the arse he's holding starts to gently lick he's shaft from bottom to top.

That's different, where's she learned that?! He gasps as the hot wet mouth surrounds his cock and starts to suck. The soft lips closing around it and starting to hit the back of her throat. It stops suddenly and she moves away leaving him empty handed.

A few seconds pass, and he notices pressure next to him pushing down into the bed. It feels slightly unstable, then there's pressure the other side of him. She's stood over him. He can feel the heat from her legs on his sides. The nylon of what ever she's wearing close to his freshly oiled skin. He feels her move and almost instantly he senses the heat from her groin hover over his large manhood. He imagines the skin tag on her perineum dangling subtly and touching the end of his cock. He starts to breath heavy.

"How do you feel, my love?" Anne asks him from above.

"Incredibly horny!"

"Good"

His penis sinks deep into her as she lowers her weight onto him, feet still supporting her. She places her hands on his chest and starts to raise her weight off of him again and just as he feels like he'll be out of her, she slams hard onto him, it almost hurts his balls, he groans aloud!

She continues to slam against him, her crotch fully open and giving her warm, slimy quim to him fully. All of a sudden, the towel is whipped away from his face.

His eyes begin to focus after being closed for so long, ahead of him sitting astride him ins't Anne. He knows now and things start to make sense. The tits he felt on him, he could have been sure were smaller, they were, and surrounded by a black see-through lace bra. Perfect as Anne's but smaller. His hand fall onto the woman's hips, he hasn't looked her in the face yet. He looks to the left. Sat in the brown leather chair in the corner, the one he was sure squeaked, is sat Anne.

He looks to her wearing green and black lace underwear. French knickers, that he loves and the bra he loves to see her dark pink nipple through. Her breasts are exposed though and she has her left breast cupped in her hand, nipple between her thumb and first finger. She's sat in shadow, only the right-hand side of her body as he looks at her is lined with candle light. Her heels are tucked up by her ass cheek and her legs spread. The right-hand lip of her trimmed pussy mound is showing, and he can see the glisten of her wetness. Her right finger is tracing its way up and down her slit, stopping to circle her clit at the top each time.

"Happy birthday my love" she speaks softly but gruffly. The horny voice he knows so well "I hope you didn't mind me inviting Diane!"

"What?!" He turns his head sharply back to the woman he's still inside of. Now her sees her fully.

Her round face and long dark hair were falling naturally from her shoulders, thinner than Anne, her ribs were visible but not too thin. Just a sexy woman.

"Anne and I discussed yours and Del's cocks ages back, and she told me yours was huge. When I told her Del's isn't, she told me I should come and have a go on yours as a joke-"

Anne cut in,

"Then after a couple of times we discussed how much she needed something bigger, even just once, so we hatched this plan. I'm sorry if it's not what you want, but I thought you kinda had a thing for Diane too. Are you ok?"

"I'm sure I'll manage" he smiled at both women. "Come here, wife, and watch your friend ride me!"

Anne stands up, her puffy lips still half exposed from touching herself. She takes a step towards her husband and kissed him upside down.

"I love you; you know!" She tells him passionately.

"I love you too" his hands fall away from Diane's hips and to Anne's face. He kisses her deeply back, and instinctively Diane starts to rock backward and forwards with his large member pushing against her insides, widening her womanhood like she'd never had before.it stung a little and she thought to herself, *Anne's pussy must be well stretched out!"*

Anne moved closer to the table, and knelt up over Stan's face. Her wet shiny clam half showing.he reached around her soft shapely leg and completed its exposure. Just inches from his face, he buried his face into his wife's tidy but very wet pussy. Her hole tasted sweet as always. She was so wet; he couldn't eat her fast enough. His face was covered in her wetness entirely. She enjoyed the roughness of his stubble along her delicate parts. She started to grind hard into his face.

She hadn't felt this aroused for a very long time. She watches intently as her husband's cock slid into her best friend and remembered the first time; she took his cock all those years ago.

She'd only popped in for coffee and within half an hour she was bent over his old tatty sofa. That was the first time she truly knew what it was to have a large dick inside her and it felt like she was a 15-year-old virgin again. She bled a little the first time, and the second and third time. But by God it was worth it.

She reached forward and put her arms on Di's shoulders, and pulled her closer.

"I'm not that way you know" Diane said coyly.

"Me either" Anne told her as she kissed her more deeply and passionately than she's ever been kissed before. They embraced and kissed gently, two women atop of a powerful but completely sub servant man. Di continued to slide up and down the considerable shaft easily as she was so wet. *I wish Del would fuck me like this!* She imagined. As Anne continues to make her husband eat her from below. Diane starts to breath heavy and Anne recognises what's happening. She reaches down to her crutch, and easily locates her best friends swollen clit. Diane bears down on the huge dick inside her and pull Anne in to kiss her. She pants and screams carnally into Anne's mouth and sucks air while trying to kiss her still. She collapses and rest her head on Anne's shoulder. Stan taps Anne's leg for air.

"Sorry my love!"

Diane started to chuckle as she realised that for the first time, she had not only cum on a cock other than her husbands, but that it belonged to her best friend who had just touched her clit and sent her over the edge whilst kissing her deeply. Did Di love Anne now? She wasn't sure.

"Oh fuck, oh fuck, oh fuck!" She said aloud. "Del's gonna fucking kill me!"

Muffled, from below his wife, came a voice belonging to the dick still inside her.

"He'll never know, unless you tell him"

"Huh" she agreed and sighed at the same time.

Anne climbed off of her husband's face, and turned to kiss him.

"I wish I could have seen that" he told her. She pointed to his right at the bookshelf and sure enough there was the iPad recording in full flow.

"For later" she told him "Now give Di a break". She clambered off of him, legs shanking and not knowing where to look. She never was great at post sex stuff. Usually, she'd empty dels muck out on the loo, in darkness and then get back into bed fully dressed. But here she was with a still horny couple, dressed in lingerie with a sore cunt from that monster cock!

“Sore?” Anne asked her.

“Yes, a bit” Di giggled

“I told you! I was too the first time he had me! Now anyway, just for my own little thing, Stan, sit there on the sofa!”.

Anne was now in full control of all parties. It wasn’t her usual role but she seemed to have settled into it nicely.

“Di, sit back on that dick, he’s not finished yet!” Stan sat on the brown leather chair. It squeaked as before, and as Diane began to straddle him, Anne stopped her.

“Turn around!” She commands her. She does as instructed, and reaches for the veiny pole between her legs, and guides it back into her already tender hole. It fits better this time, and she manages the whole length. Her small round arse rests on Stan’s pubes. He leans back to enjoy the view.

Anne pushes Di backward so she’s laying on her husband's big chest and pulls her legs apart. She wants to watch the giant shaft penetrate her friend up close. She moved in closer and takes her husband's shorn scrotum in her mouth, gently sucking on his balls. He groans deeply. As she sucks, her nose touches her friend's clit and the stretched pussy in front of her face. A devil sits on her shoulder and she answers.

“Babe!” Anne commands. “Hold her!” Stan wraps his strong arms around Di and pulls her close. He kisses her neck as he continues to penetrate her. Anne’s head moves in, she starts to kiss Di’s inner legs. Her own pussy yearning for cock now. Working her way in, before long her mouth is gently kissing her friend's outer pussy. It’s shaven, clean, and bald. Slippery with her own cum and juices. Anne tastes a woman for the first time. She’s tasted herself before and it was similar but not quite the same. Sweet and a little salty. Beautiful. She ran her tongue along both side of her slit, separated by her husband's penis. As her tongue glided along both her friend and husband, she reached between her own legs, she need penetration herself, so she slid her two middle fingers of her left hand into her own soggy cunt.

Pulling her fingers out, but not letting up from her oral duties, Anne presented her fingers to Stan. He licked them clean entirely, and then she presented the m to Di. She hesitated, but looked at her friend between her legs and took them into her mouth. Running her tongue around them absent Anne into a short frenzy of moaning. She zeroed in on Di's clit and began to suck and flick with her tongue at the same time, just like Stan does to her own hidden gem. It's too much for Di.

Her filled pussy starts to tighten around Stan's girth once again and convulse internally. The sucking and licking of her clit over whelm her and the second orgasm rises from within.

"Oh god!" She calls as Stan still hold her, and she arches once again, this time against him, spraying Anne with her juice with a giving a final shudder and jerk.

Anne kisses friends now pulsing pussy softly, pulls her husband's length from inside her and take it into her own mouth. Stopping between sucking she tells him

"Babe...........we made her..............squirt all over the place!" Di starts to chuckle as she shimmies off of Stan's lap and stands. She thinks she's finished.

"Oh, I don't think so Mrs!" Anne tells her. She turns back without a word and raises an eyebrow to her.

Anne turns to her husband.

"My turn!" Her eyes light up and he smirks silently back at her taking the time to admire her perfect curves. She pulled her French knickers down now, bending over deliberately in front of him and removes her bra exposing herself fully to her husband and her friend. She sits down on his pole, easily as she's done thousands of times before, and takes it to the hilt.

Stan turns her head and kisses her deeply.

"Thanks for my birthday present, I love it". He tells her.

Anne looks Diane in the eye as she now sits back on Stan as Di had done. She puts the tip of her finger on her little clit. It tingles a bit.

"Your turn!"

Di kneels before the married couple, now naked herself, her wedding ring catching the candle light and she starts to tentatively kiss Anne's very swollen, sensitive and very very wet pussy.

Anne is a sexual woman but this is a new level for her. Di flicks her clit with her thumb, and licks her spread and full labia gently. Stan unexpectedly starts to slide in and out of her against her own rhythm. She feels it build.

"Oh no, not yet!" Stan holds her hips and forces his whole length into her from below as Di tastes her, her juices start to leak and begins to taste them, new to her she pulls Anne's pussy into her face.

Anne finally lets it go. Her body shakes and writhes as she arched her back. Her husband holds her tight. She pulls herself up enough to get off of his piece. But she collapses on top of him. Di stands and walks up her with her hands, and kisses her deeply and passionately. Di is sure she has fallen for Anne now.

"So, are you going to finish me off then or what?" Stan asks the pair of them. He lifts Anne off of him and starts to stand.

"I know, seeing as you two are enjoying yourselves Di, lay on the sofa, babe lay on top of her and make out"

They comply willingly. Kissing each other gently, caressing each other's breasts, taking time with each other as they never had before. Stan watched for a minute, running his length up and down in his hand. He stands behind them.

Looking down in the dimness, he can still make out both of their well-used clams. Anne's was well packed and neat as always, Di had larger inner lips, but they were symmetrical like a butterfly. He moved closer, and mounting behind the women, he forced himself into Di. She gasped and Anne knew why. He loved her tightness. Clearly Del hadn't done much to fill her out. And then he swapped and slid directly into his wife. He kept going back and forth between the two women as Di continues to fall for his wife beneath him.

"Who wants my cum?" Stan asked as his pace picked up.

"Give it to Di!" Anne commanded, "I want to watch it drop from her after!"

Stan did as instruct. He slid into Di's tighter shaven gash and grabbed her by the hips. Anne was doggy style over the top of her. He held Di's ankles and forced her apart he started to pump hard and deep. It hurt her a little her insides were beginning to feel bruised. So reached up under Anne and slid two fingers into her. Stan saw it and he could no longer hold back. His balls tightened as they always do, and he felt his body start to pump his load like a pulse. His hot, sticky mess was injected deep into his wife's friend and she felt it too! His load was hot compared to her and she felt it hit her insides.

He withdrew almost immediately to see the mess he made. Anne joined him, and they hugged each other, both naked as they watched Di lay there naked, shaking but smiling with hot white mess leaking from her twat. She reached down and felt it with her hands. It felt dirty to her but that's was ok. Using her two first fingers she opens herself up so they could see into her, more of his mess spilled out.

"Get a picture then" she told them! Stan grabbed the iPad and followed the order. They joined her on the sofa and sat either side of them. All three naked and completely unashamed. Anne turned to her husband and kissed him across Di.

"Happy birthday baby" she said, Di felt a small pang of jealousy come across her.

"So, what now?" She asked the couple.

"Wine?" Stan said.

"Yes, but that's not what I meant". Di cut in, starting to feel embarrassed slightly. Anne kissed her.

"Well, now we're closer friends than we were before, and I'm ok if you're ok."

"Oh, I'm more than okay! I haven't cum like that in years. Stan, I'm going to have to jump on you from time to time, that can't be a one-time thing!" He laughed

"That's up to Anne. I belong to her and will follow instructions as necessary!"

"What about Del?" Anne quizzed.

"God knows. Maybe I'll convince him to find a girlfriend, then he'll not get curious if I'm here too often!"

"Ha maybe. You'd be happy with that?" Anne asked her.

"Oh I don't know, but I've never cum like that before! Sorry about the mess!

"Ah it's ok, we've got a vax!"

www.ingramcontent.com/pod-product-compliance
Lightning Source LLC
LaVergne TN
LVHW050338160826
845677LV00014B/3666
* 9 7 9 8 7 5 7 0 3 8 1 1 7 *